HYDROGEN

Lisa Gay

This book is a work of fiction. The names, characters, places, and incidents are either the product of the author's imagination or used factitiously. Any resemblance to an actual person, living or dead, business establishment, or event is entirely coincidental.

ISBN-13: 978-1-945858-25-3

Table of Contents

Dolphin language

** are extremely high-frequency sounds

– – are high-frequency sounds

** are mid-frequency sounds

_ _ are low-frequency sounds

Low-frequency sounds travel farther in H_2O.

Those involved in these incidents

Xanthos – Pilot and Lead Explorer.

Piminy – Science Officer.

Also known as "*************." dies on purpose

Kinion – Security Officer.

AKA ****_ _ _ **_

Talia – The spacecraft of Xanthos, Piminy, and Kinion.

Fynia - The spacecraft of Toros, Liecony, and one thousand others.

_ _ _ _ _ _ _** The name the dolphins call themselves.

–**_ _* The leader and the largest of the dolphin pod. Has several scars on its body.

AKA Victorious

– –**_ _ _** Female dolphin with a scar on its nose.

AKA Scar Nose

– – –*** –** Female dolphin with a tracking tag on the trailing edge of its dorsal fin.

AKA Tag

_ _ _ _ ** Sister of Victorius. She has no injuries.

AKA Squirt

_ _ _ _ _* –** The daughter of Tag and Victorius. She is the youngest and smallest.

AKA Little One

******– – – – – –* The orphan niece of Victorius. She has a hole in her dorsal fin.

AKA Hole in Fin

Bobby — the teenager who heard the seismograph and decided to investigate. Co-collector of the silver orb.

Stan — a friend of Bobby and co-collector of the silver orb.

Mortimer – Bobby's father.

Patrick – A video game friend of Bobby and Stan.

Michael – A video game friend of Bobby and Stan.

Karen Hollander - Commander of Guam Research Station (GRS)

Carl- The head of security at GRS.

Paul – A security guard at GRS.

Tano - A security guard at GRS.

Rai – A security guard at GRS.

Jerome -Stan's father

Betty – Stan's mother

Liecony – Chief Cephalopodan Science Officer and Piminy's parent.

Toros - Commander of the Cephalopodan consortium.

Hornion – rash volunteer

*

Water is simple

Hydrogen and oxygen

Marvels then ensue

*

Arrival

Piminy ordered, "Stop arguing with me and land!"

"This is a stupid assignment!" declared Xanthos. "It's a well-known fact that life needs hydrogen to exist. The hydrogen on this planet is bound to oxygen. We can't metabolize it."

As if the leader of their space expedition didn't already know, Piminy informed Xanthos, "We have fluorine. It will break the hydrogen covalent bond. We'll be able to absorb the freed hydrogen."

Xanthos willed their craft to decelerate.

"I'll get a container of it. I love you for trying to help my pod." Piminy's sucker pad left a spot of slime beside Xanthos's rear eye.

With that same eye, Xanthos watched Piminy will the hatch open, and a container of the hydrogen absorption enhancer to float into the space the two of them occupied.

As their craft, named Talia, bobbed on the waves of the planet, Piminy popped the container lid by thinking it. "I'm the science officer. I'll go out and analyze the environment."

An interior door formed. Ovals entered the command center. Their suction pads adhered in a circle just inside the round hole. Folded-back on themselves, long tubes that shimmered with opalescent scales slithered in until the head popped through, followed by its two upper tentacles. "You are never to go out alone, and you know it. Not even Liecony is allowed to go into an unknown environment without a security escort, and she is the Chief Science Officer." Kinion stretched its lower tentacles over the exit hatch and plastered the suckers of its head tentacles to the ceiling, effectively preventing any unauthorized exit. "I'm a security officer because my slime connection is unbreakable, so don't think you can move me, Piminy!"

"I can't save my pod if I share the glory with you." Piminy smeared fluorine on the smooth skin of a tentacle.

Kinion protested. "What about my pod?!"

"Your pod doesn't matter. Having super slime and scales everywhere means nothing! My parent and the rest of my pod will figure out a way to save our home!" Piminy's Kinion-facing mouth expanded open, showing not only its two circular rows of sharp teeth but also the inner baleen.

Kinion screamed the thought. "You're of a vain pod worthy only of contempt!"

Xanthos thought only to Kinion. "I know what you are doing. Go ahead."

"No scale! Your scales barely pass your suckers. As you said, I am entirely covered." Kinion flattened to make as wide a surface as possible and then opened its scales.

Piminy turned bright red and threw the fluorine

container at Kinion with all its thought power. The enhancer splattered over most of Kinion, who quickly closed its scales to keep the enhancer next to its smooth under skin.

Piminy snarled with wide open mouths, popped out eyes, and head suckers wound together into a hard spear.

Xanthos thought to Piminy as lovingly as it could, because Xanthos did love Piminy even though Piminy was not open to opinions that did not originate with it. "If you weren't so skinned, you wouldn't let Kinion provoke you into doing what it wants. We can save all our pods if we work together."

Kinion's scales glittered silver with pride at Xanthos's comment. Now covered in fluorine and able to absorb hydrogen from the H_2O in which Talia floated, it thought aloud, "Let's go find out if intelligent life exists here." It allowed the outer hull of Talia to rotate to the appropriate orientation.

Piminy spread its tentacles and dropped, allowing its exposed skin to absorb all the enhancer on the floor. "The intelligent life must be in the liquid we're floating on. It covers most of this planet. I'm sure we can move around in it quite well. Let's go."

Into the Liquid

Two cephalopods dropped headfirst into the ocean. "Salty! This is quite pleasant!" Piminy extended its mouths only enough for its baleen to gather small edible life, if there was any. "And rich in food!"

Kinion brought in the fluid it had jumped into, swallowed tiny krill, spread and then drew its tentacles together, and jetted through the liquid. "Piminy, you look green. Are you getting enough hydrogen?"

"I thought you would be happy if I were dead."

"No, we need you to complete this mission. We should go back to Talia."

"I'm fine. I'm trying to match the color of this liquid. I think it's beautiful."

"Stop messing around and start taking measurements."

"I have been. This is better than our home, and it's big. If we can figure out a better way to use this hydrogen, we should forget about Cephalopodia and come here. If it's safe."

"I haven't determined that yet, and nobody has figured out how to get more hydrogen back home. What makes you think Liecony or any of the rest of your pod will be able to do it here?"

"Nobody can make hydrogen. It's either there or not, and Cephalopodia is almost out. There is trillions of times more on this planet. We just need to free it up."

"All right. Let's go deeper."

They descended into a school of glittery, blue fish. Piminy matched their color and direction of travel and thought to them, "Where are you going?" but heard no reply. "I am here. Hello!" Still no reply. "I don't know how to talk to them." Piminy suddenly changed to bright red. The school of fish scattered, then reformed. "They must not be the intelligent ones. Should we go deeper, or farther, or back to Xanthos?"

"We will follow these since they are going toward Talia."

As Kinion strained the food from the surrounding liquid, the fish suddenly swam in a circle, going round and round. "They aren't going anywhere. They are definitely not what we are looking for."

Piminy changed to its normal pearly color. "They are probably doing this for a reason. I want to do what they do and see what happens." With eyes focused on the fish, Piminy swam to the far side of the Blue Jack school.

Right behind but looking ahead, Kinion warned, "Look out! A giant mouth is about to swallow you." Kinion turned bright orange and jetted past the giant's eye.

The enormous sperm whale veered to chase something orange that looked like its favorite meal. The thing resembling a giant orange squid was nowhere to be seen. An opaque, blue-green shape made no movements that weren't exactly like the substance it swam in. The owner of the giant mouth ascended to the surface, blew a fountain of H_2O out of a small hole in its back, sucked in the substance on the other side of the liquid, and then dove to search for what it thought it had seen.

Piminy asked, "Should we follow it?"

"I've never seen anything that big. We should stay far away from it. Let's get out of here." Kinion jetted toward safety, but didn't get far. A smaller, faster predator, with teeth able to rip the now visible Cephalopods to pieces, approached. "We won't be able to swim fast enough to get away from that!" Kinion made itself bright red. "Go green and get to the ship. Let them know it's too dangerous."

Jetting through the liquid as fast as it could go, Piminy screamed, "Xanthos, let me in!"

Xanthos opened the hatch. Piminy shot into the ship with so much velocity that it hit the ceiling with a thud and then dropped back through the hole. Xanthos grabbed and pulled Piminy in. "Where's Kinion?"

"Inside a monster."

Intelligent Life

Kinion formed its body into a long pole and speared toward the shark that intended to eat a red octopus. The predator had never seen prey swim directly toward it. Slightly confused, it slowed but opened its mouth just the same. Even though Kinion was not even half the size of the one trying to eat it, the two of them swam straight toward each other. At the last second, Kinion veered upward and over. Once past the long teeth, it extended its tentacles, wrapped them around the ravenous creature, and then slapped its sucker pads against the smooth skin. The strong slime of the warrior pod kept it attached to the killer as it rolled and thrashed. As soon as Kinion experienced a millisecond of stillness, it glued its head tentacles to the beast to stop the stress against its limbs caused by its head flinging about. Afraid they would get ripped off, Kinion kept all its mouths and eyes drawn tightly into its head.

The noise from the trashing sent sound waves through the liquid, which usually meant a land dweller had fallen into the ocean. A nearby pod of natives decided to help.

Echolocation pings from those coming to Kinion's aid registered in Kinion's severely shaken head. The sounds grew louder, and then a sleek aquatic mammal rammed its long, hard nose into the body of the one Kinion clung to. Its rescuers appeared to carefully avoid injuring Kinion's soft tentacles. Kinion's attacker tried to get away. Kinion drew its sucker pads in, allowing the creature to slip out of its limbs. The six mammals that had come to Kinion's aid circled, making clicking sounds.

That must be how they communicate. I don't know what they're saying. Kinion tried to imitate the sound.

The dolphins echoed each sound that Kinion made. However, no progress was made in understanding each other. *This is clearly the intelligent species on this planet. How will we learn to understand each other?* Fascinated, Kinion paid no attention to the amount of hydrogen it had been absorbing, but was no longer. Suddenly, Kinion strained to maintain its color. *My enhancer must be used up.* Kinion clicked rapidly, turned translucent, and then tried to swim to the ship. *I'm too far away. I don't think I'll make it!* No longer able to absorb hydrogen, it slowed. "I can't move!" it exclaimed, then stopped. "I was stupid!" Kinion thought no longer.

Kinion's might-have-been-saviors pushed Kinion's motionless body toward the object whose impact had drawn them to this part of the vast H_2O expanse.

Piminy swam toward the group, thought screamed, "Kinion!" then realized that the animals knew Kinion needed help and were trying to get it to the ship. It seemed that it was too late. The local inhabitants swam circles around the cephalopods, clicking.

Then, the vestigial slits just below Kinion's head tentacles opened. As the H_2O flowed through the openings, Kinion's scales turned progressively whiter until they gleamed pearly cream. Its eyes opened. "Is this the afterlife? I remember that I died."

"You did, or almost did. But your head slits opened. For eons, nobody believed they could work. I guess they've never had to, until you couldn't absorb hydrogen through your skin. The myth that Cephalopodia was once covered in liquid must be true."

"That was the worst and scariest feeling I've ever had, and I never want to go through that again."

"But now you're free! You don't need to pay for fluorine. At least not while you're here. I wonder if you can do both, or maybe you can't absorb hydrogen through your skin anymore."

"Let's go find out, but first, I want you to meet the intelligent life on this planet. I haven't figured out exactly how to communicate with them. Kinion spoke a melody of clicks, "−**_ _*," and pointed toward a specific dolphin, "And this is, −−**_ _ _**." The next limb pointed at a different one. Each dolphin was named and responded by repeating the clicks produced by Kinion. With its gills opened, Kinion heard the sounds more clearly, or perhaps it felt them as well.

Piminy pulled itself into the ship through the hatch. Kinion tried to signal to its saviors to stay by pointing to them, then to itself, and finally all of them together, before indicating the space beside the ship. Through the clear sides of their ship with the space shields open, the three cephalopods watched the dolphins play, hunt fish, and swim nearby.

Kinion's gills closed. Its skin absorbed the hydrogen pumped into the command cabin. "I hope my gills open again if I go back into the liquid."

"What was it like? I mean, dying," Piminy asked.

"Awful! Just pure awful!"

Xanthos told its shipmates, "I would find it hard to die on purpose."

Dying on Purpose

"How do we protect ourselves while we are dead?" Piminy inquired. "We should not assume those creatures will help us."

"Let me see if I can find a way to ask them if they will." Kinion opened the exit portal, dropped into the H_2O, and was elated when its gills immediately opened.

The dolphins swam to their new friend. Kinion made the clicks it believed meant the name of the largest of the group, "–**_ _*," and was elated when that was the one who responded. Once again, Kinion made the same clicks and touched the dolphin he thought belonged to the name. The others bobbed their heads up and down. Kinion pointed to itself. All the locals made the melody of clicks, "****_ _ _ **_." Kinion repeated, "****_ _ _ **_," and touched itself. The dolphins bobbed their heads. Kinion said, "–**_ _*," which it thought meant the large dolphin, but touched itself. The dolphins shook their heads from side to side, then touched the one Kinion thought matched the clicks. Kinion touched each dolphin, listened to their names, and repeated them. It touched all six of the locals and waited. They clicked their name for their species, "_ _ _ _ _ _ _ **."

Kinion knew it could learn their language. It swam and then waited for the locals to click the word "swim." Kinion thought and clicked "swim." Next, it floated as if again dead, learned the clicks for that word, and passed them on to its fellow space travelers. Kinion thought to those in the ship, "I don't know how to demonstrate the predator or the help the locals gave, but I figured out how to learn their language. Do you want to come out and learn?"

"One of us should stay inside the ship. I am the science officer," Piminy looked at Xanthos.

Xanthos authorized the request, "Go on, but for now, the two of you need to stay right beside our ship."

Piminy thought to all, "Let me put on enhancer before I go out," then applied a small amount. Piminy usually decided for itself what it would do, even though Xanthos was the leader.

Kinion thought out loud and clicked, "My name is: "**** _ _ _ **_. They are called: _ _ _ _ _ _ _ **. Their individual names are: −**_ _*. Kinion touched the largest of the pod. It looks like it has survived many battles. We can say the name means Victorious. And this is − −**_ _ _**. Kinion indicated the _ _ _ _ _ _ _ ** with a scar on its nose. I think this one's name is Scar Nose. The tip of − − −*** −**'s dorsal fin is notched, and something is stuck in it. Let's call it Tag. **_ _ _ _ has no injuries. I saw it squirt H_2O out of its back. We should name it Squirt. _ _ _ _ _* −** is the smallest. She is Little One. ******− − − − − −* has a hole in its dorsal fin, so we will call it Hole in Fin."

Piminy touched itself.

The _ _ _ _ _ _ _ ** shook their heads sideways.

"I guess I don't have a name." Which was acceptable to Piminy for the moment.

The two cephalopods and the six _ _ _ _ _ _ _ ** demonstrated, clicked, and learned many words as they swam farther and farther from the spaceship.

Kinion noticed Piminy growing pale. "How much fluorine did you put on?"

"Not much. I want to be able to breathe in this H_2O."

"It might not work for you, and we're too far away to get you back to hydrogen! You can't allow anybody else to do something you can't. Your vanity is going to kill you," were the last words Piminy heard.

Kinion pulled the unconscious, arrogant cephalopod as fast as possible and broadcast its thoughts to Xanthos to hyper-saturate the ship with hydrogen.

The rush of liquid flowing past Piminy's closed gills sprang them open even faster than Kinion's. Piminy felt itself jetting through the liquid, felt hydrogen coursing through its body, and then opened its eyes. The _ _ _ _ _ _ _ **'s raced at its sides. It pointed an eye forward. There was Kinion. Just to be sure they weren't trying to escape another predator, Piminy looked behind them with its fourth eye. Only the beautiful blue-green liquid vastness and its own coral-colored body came into view. "Have you seen me? I'm lovely!"

Kinion stopped. "I should kill you again for doing that to me!" Kinion looked at the gorgeous, shimmering coral cephalopod. "However, you are lovely."

"Thank you. I think so too. I can't wait for Xanthos to see me."

"Ughh," thought Kinion all to itself. Then told Piminy, "You go in and explain what you did while I wait outside the ship. I don't want to watch Xanthos kill you."

"I am a science officer, and this was an experiment. It's better to test dying on purpose on oneself than on another."

Victorius swam to Kinion. He clicked, "**************.", which in dolphins means: dies on purpose.

Test Three

Xanthos colored up to the brightest shade of red that Piminy had ever seen. "There are only three of us. You can't be replaced! I ought to scale you completely!"

To which Piminy replied, "Aren't I lovely!"

"If you ever purposely endanger the mission again, I will remove your scales one by agonizing one!" However, Xanthos silently thought, *Extremely lovely*.

Piminy continued as if Xanthos hadn't just threatened the worst possible fate. "I wonder what color you will be when your gills open."

"I am not going to kill myself! What if it doesn't work? And this planet is too dangerous for us, anyway."

"The _ _ _ _ _ _ _ **s will protect us."

"If all of us came here, there might not be enough of them, and I'm sure they have their own lives. We're fun for now. We can't expect them to do nothing but protect us, nor should we depend on anything but ourselves, and we don't know how to live in this vast expanse."

"It won't be me. You will be the one to cause us to fail our mission. We can't truly know if it's safe if we only explore the small space around the ship, and you haven't left the ship even once."

"I am the thinker and planner. I have to stay safe to do my job!"

Piminy's eye extended to the end of its stalk. To better stare down Xanthos, the inner eyelid slid away. "Scaleless!"

Xanthos faded to orange as the yellow of embarrassment seeped into its skin.

Kinion heard every thought its companions had screamed at each other and replied, "Right now, the _ _ _ _ _ _ _ **s are here," to Xanthos only.

"I'll go, but I AM staying right here with the hatch open." The hydrogen-absorption-enhancer flask floated across the command module. Xanthos applied everything inside and then dropped into the H_2O outside the ship.

Little One squeaked, "Are you afraid?" because Xanthos's fear-flooded skin glowed bright yellow.

Xanthos's tentacles twitched. "Yes."

"We love to play! We will keep the predators away if you will join us?"

"I will."

They swam upward as fast as possible, jetted into the mostly O_2 gas above the H_2O, and then splashed back into the liquid. The enhancer wore off faster than expected. Suddenly, Xanthos couldn't break the surface and then noticed its color draining away. "I don't want to be test three! I'm going back into the pod!"

Cephalopods and dolphins alike looked toward the spacecraft. The waves created by the preceding three hours had driven it away. Kinion listened for the locator. "I'll go as fast as I can and get our craft. Drag Xanthos toward it to conserve hydrogen."

Piminy slid two leg tentacles into the opening

between Xanthos's stuck-together head appendages and then around Xanthos's body. Together, they made a single spear. While Xanthos faded, Piminy used its other six legs to propel itself. When Xanthos's head tentacles loosened, Piminy clutched Xanthos's body tighter, swam, and swam, and swam. "Where are you?!" Piminy screamed at Kinion, who had just gotten into their pod.

"I'm coming to you now!"

"Xanthos's gills aren't opening!"

Kinion arrived many minutes beyond the time that it had taken for Piminy's and Kinion's gills to open. Xanthos floated colorless and flaccid in the H_2O. "Get Xanthos in. Maybe we can restart the hydrogen exchange!" Kinion flooded the command module with dense hydrogen.

Piminy jetted through the opening with Xanthos inside its tentacles. The dolphins swam circles around the pod.

Kinion had the blowers on high to dry the liquid from Xanthos's skin. "I see now that bare skin has its advantages."

"I have some enhancer." Piminy hurried to get the jar of fluorine that it had illegally and secretly brought on the trip.

"We'll talk about that later. Start rubbing it on." Kinion grabbed a tentacle and a glob of enhancer.

Piminy wailed, "I'm sorry I made Xanthos go in. Have any of us ever been revived?"

"Not this long after." Kinion rubbed enhancer on tentacle after tentacle. Nothing changed. Kinion violently flapped Xanthos' tentacles. "Absorb, you scaleless, short-tentacled, five-legged, no good— Is Xanthos looking a little colored to you?"

"Slightly urchin!"

An eye that dangled from Xanthos opened. The gaping mouth below it closed.

"By the great hydrogen maker! I think Xanthos is coming back!" exclaimed Piminy.

Several minutes of shaking Xanthos's tentacles pumped hydrogen to its brain. All Xanthos's eyes opened, and mouths closed, but it couldn't think, didn't understand where it was, or what had happened. It lay on the pod's floor, dazed.

Kinion ordered, "Keep flapping the tentacles!"

Piminy did so, along with Kinion. More hydrogen flowed into Xanthos's brain.

Suddenly, Xanthos thought, "Stop! You're about to jerk me apart!"

Piminy wrapped all its tentacles around Xanthos. "Thank the great hydrogen maker! I was afraid that we'd lost you."

Xanthos stated, "So, apparently not everybody's gills will open. That's unfortunate!"

Something Cometh

In response to Piminy stealing and illegally stowing an extra jar of hydrogen absorption enhancer, Kinion sentenced Piminy to gathering krill for Xanthos. Scar Nose swam alongside. Piminy asked, "How did you get that injury?"

Scar Nose replied, "Land dweller needed help. Coral injured thing it moves on. Sharks smelled leaking fluid. Many came. – –**_ _ _** injured fighting. Other land dweller got injured out."

"What is land dweller?"

"We in ocean. Land dweller not in ocean. On land."

"Can we see land?"

"Many lights and darks to land."

"You take us?"

"Not good you go. Feel that?"

"Feel what?"

Scar Nose tried to explain that the H_2O was vibrating.

Piminy didn't grasp the meaning of Scar Nose's clicks. That is, at first, until the pulsing in the H_2O grew stronger. "What comes?"

"Land dwellers. We go to pod."

Bobby piloted the speedboat. "I'm telling you. Stan, something crashed into the ocean. The seismic buoy recorded it. We'll be the ones to find it."

"Probably just space junk that fell." Stan scanned

the horizon with his spyglass. "I see something glittering. Go that way." Stan pointed.

In the H_2O below, Piminy and Scar Nose tried to keep up. Piminy screamed its thoughts ahead. "Sink the pod."

"I'm not leaving you or Kinion," replied Xanthos.

"Land dwellers are coming! Leave us! Sink the pod!"

Xanthos refused. "No, but I am closing the shields."

"Ready the net." Bobby circled the silver orb bobbing on the ocean. "Throw the net over it. We can drag it to the research station."

Stan's firm grip easily secured one corner of the net to the boat's handrail. He slung the rest of it toward the object the teenagers wanted to capture. It landed on top and then slid off. "I'll try again."

After many failed capture attempts, Piminy and Scar Nose arrived. They stayed under the boat. Piminy hollered, "Kinion! Come back now!"

"I'm going to jump in and pull the net around it." Bobby pulled his T-shirt off and kicked the shoes from his feet before he dove in. He thought he saw an octopus and a dolphin swim into the depths of the ocean from below his boat. *What?!*

Bobby shot back to the surface. Like a merman, his long black hair floated on the smooth ocean. "I think I saw a dolphin and an octopus together."

"You did not. They don't do that. Stop messing around and get the net around this thing."

Bobby circled the pod and handed the free end to

Stan. "I'll swim under and get the net all the way around." He disappeared again.

Bobby had encircled the spaceship with the net when Piminy heard Kinion inform its fellow space explorers, "I'm almost there!"

"We've got it. It was so hard because it's a perfect sphere. I don't think we have anything like this orbiting the planet." Bobby swam toward the ladder at the rear of the boat.

Stan turned on the motors. "Something strange IS happening. After they condemned Dock F, everybody is talking."

"Maybe a war started and nobody is telling us. I heard that a missile system is being installed." Bobby climbed in.

"Why? We're just a research station." Stan eased the throttle forward.

Bobby grabbed a towel and plopped into a seat. "Or are we?"

Piminy jetted to the ship and pulled at the tightening ropes.

"You can't free it. Get away or you will be hurt," warned Scar Nose.

"I can't let them take it. Xanthos is inside!"

As the orb picked up speed, Kinion knocked Piminy away and plastered every sucker of its body to the spaceship with the stickiest slime it could excrete. Attached to the ship, Kinion sped toward land. "I'll keep broadcasting. Find us, Piminy!"

Xanthos screamed, "Why did you leave Piminy? You should have stayed."

"Piminy can use the hydrogen in the H_2O and is with the _ _ _ _ _ _ _ ** s."

Piminy, Scar Nose, and the others of the pod could not maintain the necessary speed. Long before they could discover where the land dwellers were going, they lost sight of and the vibration of the boat, and Piminy could no longer perceive Kinion's thoughts.

Dock F

Bobby's hair flapped in the wind. "Slow down, Stan! We're in the no-wake zone."

"If I slow down too fast, the orb will run into the back of us." Stan throttled down. "Let me know if it's getting too close."

Kinion tested the net's webbing. "My mouth can fit through. When we are slow enough, open the hatch, so I can come inside."

Xanthos flushed yellow. "I'm glad you were able to hold on. I don't know what they're going to do to us."

The space pod barely moved as it floated behind the speed boat of the land dwellers. Xanthos opened the way in. Kinion spaced its mouths one behind the other and quickly squeezed through the net.

Xanthos thought the hatch closed as the two cephalopods wrapped their tentacles around each other. "I can't hear Piminy. Can you?"

"Not for a long time."

"I'm worried. I love Piminy."

Kinion thought aloud, "I know you do." In Kinion's mind alone, it said, *I do too.*

Bobby flipped a switch on the boat's console. "Dad, I have something. Come to Dock F."

"I'm busy right now, son. And why do you want me to come to the enclosed dock? It's condemned."

"So, it can't get away. Trust me. This is way more important than anything else."

"I'll lose my job if I walk away from this experiment."

"No, you won't. You'll get a promotion, but I can take the credit myself."

As if his son didn't know enough to have already completely enclosed the dock, and because he always had to have the last word, Mortimer instructed, "Make sure you close the underwater hatch too."

Bobby looked at Stan. "He'll say something else. Watch," then spoke into the microphone. "Bring the key to the crane."

"I'll have to walk all the way to the office."

"I know." Bobby turned to his friend. "Why does he think I'm stupid?"

"You better have something good."

Bobby let his father have the last word.

Stan double checked the net between the boat and the object they had collected. "It's the nature of a parent. Mine treats me the same way."

Kinion activated the sonar of the pod to investigate the space where the ship had stopped. "This isn't good. We're closed in. We're captured."

Several minutes later, the upper door of Dock F clanged open. Mortimer made his way along the walkway of a rusty, warped metal pier that rose from the ocean shelf. "I'll start the crane. What is that? Where did you get it? Attach the corners of the net to the hook." His footsteps sent vibrations into the water.

Xanthos shimmered yellow. "Whatever is out there

28

swims strangely. Double thumps. It might be another intelligent species, but I don't think they're friendly."

An unknown clanking vibrated in the water. The ship sounded, "general quarters," into the minds of its occupants.

The pod rose several feet, stopped with a loud clang, and then swung to the walkway.

Kinion was perplexed. "We're airborne? How can that be? The engine isn't running."

Mortimer jumped down from the crane control box. "Come up here, boys."

The land dwellers stood beside the perfect sphere. Bobby disclosed, "I saw the seismograph record a large impact. Before I erased it, I printed the recording and coordinates. What do you think it is?"

Impacts from Mortimer's knocks on the orb reverberated inside the ship. "It sounds hollow."

Stan postulated, "It could be part of the space station."

"We would have heard about it if the space station had lost a part, and I'm pretty sure it doesn't have anything like this. So, nobody else knows about this?"

"No, that's why I came to the abandoned dock. We can keep it a secret until we decide what it is and what to do with it."

Mortimer spoke the first praise Bobby had ever heard from his father. "Good thinking, son. Just in case somebody does come in here, let's cover it."

"Everybody's afraid to come in here since the commander condemned the dock, but I'll get a canvas," Stan started away. "What mangled this dock anyway?"

Xanthos asked for their craft's findings. The spaceship reported, "Just before three four-tentacled aliens entered this space, a small opening formed. It closed immediately after their entry. The aliens move on two tentacles and swing two by their sides. They communicate with sound waves. Two of them got back into the craft that dragged us here. One used a huge device to pull us up. We are dangling above the H_2O. They moved back to the place that opened. It opened again, and they disappeared."

Kinion asked, "How far are we above the liquid?"

"Three tentacles."

"I can drop out, reconnoiter, and then shoot up to get back in."

Xanthos instructed Kinion, "If any aliens return while you are out there, camouflage yourself."

"Of course." Kinion thought the hatch open and dropped through the hole. Its gills opened.

A quick swim around the edge of the box that contained them revealed a weak current and krill in the H_2O. The H_2O inside their prison was twelve tentacles deep. The floor was a bent metal mesh through which the krill entered and left with the current.

Kinion looked at the lattice. "I don't think I can get out. The spaces in this material are about the size of a sucker." Kinion tried to force a mouth through the diamond shaped space. A small portion of flesh ripped. "I can't get through. Maybe Piminy can. If all of us were on the ship, we could leave."

"We aren't. What else can you discover?"

Kinion's sucker slime adhered well to the long, slender rail beside a series of short horizontal ledges. It made its way up to a long horizontal ledge with vertical and horizontal rails. Kinion didn't get far before it needed hydrogen. It rolled under the lowest horizontal rail and dropped into the H_2O below. Kinion ordered the ship, "Show me where the aliens entered."

Talia emitted a laser that bored a hole through the canvas and then a microscopic depression in the door.

Kinion ascended the set of short horizontal ledges under the alien entry portal, then ran its suckers over the indicated area. "The walls up here are solid, but this part seems to be cut through. I don't know how the aliens managed to open it. I've been telling it to open, but it hasn't." One of Kinion's tentacles pushed down on a protrusion from the wall. The cutout section of the wall remained closed. "I made something move. I'm pushing on it, but nothing is happening."

The ship informed, "It opened into this room."

Due to the opening's previous non-compliance with its metal commands, Kinion pulled hard. The door swung open and knocked Kinion from the walkway. Kinion popped back to the surface of the H_2O, again made its way up the ledges, and then extended an eye into the space on the other side of the now open door. "Only a long tube with pointed edges. Why do these aliens make everything this shape? The space the ship is trapped in is the same. Nothing is our shape. In Cephalopodia, everything is beautifully round. These aliens are different from the H_2O dwellers."

Xanthos ordered, "Put the wall back the way it was and come back to the ship."

Long Distance Communication

Piminy clicked to Scar Nose, "What am I going to do? How will I find them?"

Scar Nose replied, "Whales can speak across long distances. We could ask them to help."

"What are whales? Are they safe? A monster tried to eat **** _ _ _ ** _."

"That was a shark. Whales are much bigger."

"BIGGER?!?!"

"Yes, but they eat krill, not you."

"Follow me." Victorius started toward the Oceanway, where whales return for winter breeding. It wasn't long before Piminy and the dolphins came across an old Humpback whale.

Piminy reported, "I saw something like this when we first got here. I thought it was going to eat me."

"This kind won't, but some do," Victorius requested, "Would you ask your fellow whales if any of them have seen a land dweller boat pulling a large shiny orb?"

"Why should I?" The whale had never been asked for such a thing in the past.

Victorius explained that another, like Piminy, was inside the orb and needed help.

"How quickly do you need to find it? Talking is slow for Humpback whales."

"As soon as we can, but while we are waiting for replies, we could start toward the islands." Victorious asked, "Would you come with us?"

"It's time for the other half of my brain to sleep."

"If you will ask, we will wait until you are ready and watch for danger while you sleep."

"I agree. You dolphins keep watch." The Humpback surfaced, blew a fountain of water as it exhaled through its blowhole, drew fresh air into its lungs, descended, emitted a song of low-frequency sounds, and then floated vertically.

Piminy ate krill, and her friends ate mackerel as they circled and protected the whale. About thirty minutes later, the dolphins and the whale heard a reply. The Humpback came fully awake and informed the group, "Seen at Big Island. I want to see this thing. I'm ready to travel."

"Stick yourself to me," Victorius instructed Piminy. "We will swim fast for a long time. Don't cover my blowhole."

Piminy attached itself, changed to dolphin gray, and hung on tight.

The whale that led them asked for and received updates as the group traveled. A whale close to the island assured them, "The object was taken to the island with the building that extends into the ocean. They have it inside. The ocean door is closed."

Squirt, the sister of the dolphin that carried Piminy, passed the information on.

"I still need to get there. Ask them to keep watch in case they take my ship somewhere else."

Sneaking About

Mortimer called Stan's father. "Bobby wants Stan to spend the night with us."

"Stan told me. Thanks for reaching out to me. He's getting his bag ready. He'll be over soon." Stan's father hung up the phone. "What do you two have planned? When will you get home?"

Stan lied. "We're in an online video game contest. It could take days."

"Good luck. I hope you two win, but don't wear out your welcome. Let me know how it's going. Love you, son."

Stan didn't know if something would go horribly wrong because of the orb. In case he never got to speak with his family again, he expressed his feelings. "Love you too and tell Mom I love her."

"You haven't told me you love me since you were twelve. It's nice to hear you say it."

"Of course, I love you. Just don't expect me to say it in front of anybody." Stan walked away from his family's suite.

At the end of the corridor, he turned toward Bobby and Mortimer's place.

The packs, with what Bobby and Mortimer believed they would need, sat just inside their door. Bobby's mother had been gone for over a year. They wouldn't have to explain to anybody where they were going or why.

Stan dropped his bag on the floor beside them. "Are we waiting until lights out?"

"Yes," Mortimer cautioned, "Everybody will be in their suites after lights out. We should be able to get to Dock F unobserved."

"I wish we had found this thing last week." Stan picked up the controller that he had brought with him. "*Kalagon's Edge* just came out. Patrick and Michael are expecting us to play with them."

"We've got a few hours before lights out, but then we're going to have a real adventure. Besides, we can play this game all we want when we get home."

Bobby and Stan put on their headsets and joined their friends from Virginia in the multiplayer video game.

Mortimer squirted penetrating oil on the wheels of the cart he had brought home. *We need to be quiet as we make our way tonight.* The lubricant went everywhere. He rolled the wheels back and forth until he had worked out all the salty air rust. *No Squeaks. Perfect. Just in case.* Mortimer unscrewed the air vent cover in his room. He quietly slipped to the empty suite down the hall and stepped inside. He removed the screws from the vent in the main bedroom and then crawled through the wall to his quarters.

Eleven in the evening arrived. Mortimer knocked on Bobby's door. "It's time."

"Can't stop right now. We just got to the sky kingdom. If we don't kill this boss, we have to start over on Earth." Bobby threw a magic spell and told his friends, "Dad says it's enough game for the night. When we kick the butt of this level's guard, we have to go."

"My dad is screaming at me, too." Michael dealt a devastating multi-slash to Kalagon's minion.

"At least you have dads." Patrick landed a spinning jump kick at the same time.

The talak exploded in a blast of lightning. The four players collected the items scattered across the virtual floor.

"Good game! I don't know when we'll be back. Play without us." Bobby took off his headset. "Let's go!"

Mortimer pulled the door shut behind the three orb captors. "Don't make a sound."

As they traveled the labyrinth between the living suites wing and the condemned dock, none of them noticed the deposit on the floor each time oil dripped from the chassis onto a wheel.

Something's Wrong

At Dock F, the door swung open. Talia sounded, "General Quarters."

"What's happening?" Kinion asked.

"The wall is opening," reported the spacecraft.

Xanthos issued instructions. "Record everything without emitting sound waves. Running narrative to us."

"Awesome. We made it here unseen." Bobby stepped just inside the door, took a second step onto the walkway, then attempted to lift his rear foot. It couldn't rise from the mesh below his shoe. "What the?! I can't move!" he exclaimed.

Talia thought to its inhabitants. "One is coming in."

"Come back," his father directed.

Bobby tried. "I can't move either way." He jerked his foot out of the shoe, which sent him falling forward. Fortunately, he grabbed the rail before going over.

Talia stated, "The alien ripped off the bottom of a tentacle."

"Oh no!" exclaimed Xanthos.

Stan touched the floor with a piece of paper from the notepad they had brought. "Is your hand stuck?"

"No," replied Bobby.

Mortimer told his son how to extricate himself. "Untie your shoe laces, then reach back and take my hand." Once he held his son's hand securely, he said, "Put your foot on the back shoe, take the front one out of the shoe, then I'll pull you into the hall."

Bobby got set. "Now, Dad." Mortimer and Stan pulled. Bobby fell backward onto the hall floor. "That thing must be emitting some kind of gas that turns to glue."

In a statement of the facts, Talia reported, "It reversed back toward the opening. Some tentacles extended in, grabbed the alien, and pulled it out. The bottoms of two tentacles are still on the walkway."

"They are too fragile," Kinion commented.

Xanthos pondered, "I wonder why that happened. It didn't the last time they came in."

"It can't be a gas," Stan replied, "The railing wasn't glued." He stuck small pieces of paper all around the door. "The floor to the side of the door is clear. I'm going to step on Bobby's shoes and test the other side of the walkway." Stan held the rail where Bobby had tried to stick paper, then leaned down to test the walkway. "We can get around this gluey part if we step on Bobby's shoes."

The orb suspended on the other side of the dock informed its occupants, "The ends of their short tentacles have five small tentacles. The tentacle ends of one of the aliens have something thin and flat that they're pressing against the walkway."

"It must be a test strip of some kind," Xanthos thought to Kinion and the ship.

"What are they doing now? Are they coming this way? I'll fight them if I have to." Kinion whipped its head tentacles into a spear.

"There are three aliens. One has bent its two long tentacles. It's rubbing the test strip on the walkway. It's not sticking. The other two are coming toward us. It will be a long time before they get here. They don't move fast when they become short."

Mortimer knew what to do first, given the new development. "We will probably go through this whole pad of paper testing everywhere. That's probably all we'll be able to do tonight. We can come back tomorrow with something to put on the sticky places. Bobby, you test going toward the ocean door. Stan, test the stairs. I'll start down the long way."

They each wrapped a piece of paper around their hands and started in. Stan put his hand on the rail to see if he could swing past the glue on the floor. The paper stuck. He got a new sheet and reached under the rail to the step. "Stairs aren't usable. Glue everywhere. How are you guys doing?"

Bobby answered, "Nothing on the floor or railing so far."

"Same," said Mortimer. "Stan, help going this way."

At the end of the short walkway toward the ocean, Bobby turned back. *I wonder if sheets of paper would be enough to keep us from sticking.* He touched a second sheet of paper to the one stuck to the handrail going down to the ocean. "Awesome." He covered the section at the door, but still walked across on his stuck-down shoes. His father and Stan had gotten halfway down the long section. Bobby walked to them. "It seems one sheet of paper might be enough to stop the glue."

"Behind the door is sticky. Tomorrow, we'll bring something heavy and expendable and test your theory."

Several feet from the crane, the floor became sticky again. The rail was not gluey, so they slipped along on the bottom rail until the stairs. Stan offered, "Hold my hand. I'll reach across and test the rail on the other side."

Mortimer refused, "No, I don't want you stuck. You hold me, and I'll test." He stepped around Stan, held his hand tight, leaned, tapped a sheet of paper to the far rail, and then raised his hand. The paper slid off and wafted back and forth as it dropped to the water below. He tested the lower rail, which was much harder since he had to lean out and down. It didn't stick either. "I'm going across."

On the far side, Mortimer squatted on the lower rail while holding the upper one. He pushed a corner of the paper to the floor and then attempted to move it. It also floated off into the air. "I think this side is clear." He placed his foot in the test spot and proceeded onward.

With all the testing of the upper floor complete, they were done. Mortimer sighed, "We can't get to the lower level. Both stairs are infected. It's a good thing we already got this up here."

"What do you think left the glue?" Bobby asked.

Stan knocked on the orb. "I think something came out of this, went up the stairs on both sides, and a short way down this catwalk. Wherever it goes, it leaves this sticky slime. I think there are space slugs inside."

"SPACE SLUGS!" Bobby laughed. "Space slugs? There aren't space slugs."

Stan's face turned red. "How do you know what is or isn't out there?"

The ship stated its conclusion, "It's established, Kinion. The slime you excrete stops them."

Kinion knew what that meant. "If they get our ship open, I'll slime them."

Xanthos flushed bright yellow. "Great Hydrogen Maker, save us!"

Talia alerted its occupants of its plan. "I'm going to take off and blast out of here."

"NO! THAT'S AN ORDER!" Kinion believed it could overcome the aliens and didn't want to leave Piminy.

Mortimer thought about Stan's idea. *Something did this, and it's a good bet it's something inside the sphere.* "We'd better go."

Once the aliens had vacated Dock F, as the leader and also as a scared Cephalopod, Xanthos ordered Kinion, "Go out and cover everything with slime."

"Incoming message." Talia relayed the dispatch. "All on way. Only enough hydrogen to your current location, equidistant, or closer planet. Send report."

Xanthos spoke its opinion. "It doesn't seem safe here, but there wasn't enough hydrogen anywhere else."

"We don't need to answer immediately." Talia opened the hatch. "Go slime everything."

Kinion dropped out and spent the entire light period of this strange and hostile planet oozing goo on every surface of their prison.

On the way home, the land dwellers still didn't notice the oil in the hall left by the cart's first pass or the return trip. Once safely inside Mortimer's suite, they fell into bed and dreamed nightmares of space slugs.

The Trench

Piminy and friends jetted through the H_2O. Just when it seemed that they were rapidly traveling a vast expanse, one of the dolphins or the whale had to let half its brain sleep. When the dolphins did so, they continued swimming but at a much slower rate. When the whale slept, they stopped.

Piminy fretted and tried its best, with its limited knowledge of the language of dolphins, to explain, "Others like Kinion, Xanthos, and I needed a new place to live—one with an abundant supply of hydrogen that would be safe for our species. We have soft bodies. Things here can kill us. Is there another part of this H_2O that doesn't have land dwellers or sharks or other vicious things trying to eat us?"

Since the whale was half awake, surfacing every few minutes to breathe, it answered. "The trench. Very few things down there, but the pressure is extreme. I can only go partway down."

Piminy asked, "Is it close? I can experiment on myself. I do it all the time."

Squirt answered, "We will pass over it today. But I thought you need to get to your ship as fast as possible."

The whale woke. "I saw a small octopus very deep. They look a lot like you. You might live down there."

"We can go down and back up in minutes," said Victorius.

Piminy glowed purple with joy. "The trench might be the answer." It faded to yellow. "But Xanthos can't breathe this liquid. Some of us will die."

The group swam alternately rapidly, then slowly while dolphins slept, until the next sleep of the whale. Squirt informed Piminy, "We are halfway across. We should test here. How will I know if you can't go farther down?"

"I will become clear."

Victorious advised Piminy, "Hold on to me." Then told Tag, "You watch "************·". Let me know if it starts to turn clear."

Tag cautioned her mate, "I should carry "************·". You swim so fast, I won't be able to keep up. We can stay together if you don't pass me."

Piminy changed to its brightest shade of red, wrapped its tentacles around, and glued its suckers to its choice. "I'll ride – – –*** –**. Let's go."

Down they went. When the light started to dim, Tag asked, "************·", "Are you falling off? Your tentacles aren't going all the way around me anymore."

Piminy noticed that Tag was correct and grabbed tighter. *Am I shrinking, or is* Tag *expanding?* As the H_2O grew darker, Piminy's tentacles became shorter and shorter.

In the ocean twilight zone, Piminy looked gray. Victorious instructed Piminy, "Change to blue."

Piminy did so. "Am I clear?"

"You still have plenty of color, but you are much smaller."

Down they went. When it was quite dark, Piminy's suckers glowed green. It saw that its entire body was only a tenth as wide as its ride. "I'm shrinking and glowing!"

Not much farther down, Tag stated, "You might be able to go down farther, but I can't."

"Turn back. Have we passed all predators?"

Victorius answered, "Mostly, and land dwellers don't come here. We don't know what is deeper."

As they ascended, Piminy's suckers returned to pink and its body to its original size. "We did have a predator on Cephalopodia. We killed most of them. That's when the hydrogen started disappearing. I told them to stop killing them. I told them they were making the hydrogen, but nobody listened to me. Anyway, once I get to my friends, we will come back and see what's down there."

What to say

When Kinion returned, Xanthos conveyed its opinion on the contents of their report. "We should state all the facts and leave the decision to come or not up to them."

"All the facts is too much data to transmit," said Kinion.

For the first time, the ship did not simply do as it was told. Talia pointed out an important fact. "We already sent full reports on all previous planets. We only need to report what we know about this one."

"First, we'll transmit all our experiences to Talia. The ship can compile everything into the shortest message that conveys all the necessary information. You can do that, can't you, Talia?"

"Before I transmit, we should wait and see if Piminy finds us. We need that information. I will read you first, Xanthos."

Xanthos shielded its personal thoughts about Piminy. "Go ahead."

Kinion also hid thoughts about Piminy before allowing Talia access to its mind.

Talia stopped receiving after only a few minutes. "There are gaps in both your records. What are you hiding?"

"Personal thoughts," Kinion replied. "They aren't relevant to our mission."

"I decide what's relevant. That's what Xanthos just told me to do." Talia continued, "I don't withhold information from any of you."

Xanthos had never seen their ship offended, wondered what else Talia might do differently, and secretly thought, *Will Talia abandon us?*

"I will never abandon you," Talia replied indignantly.

"You heard that?" Xanthos exclaimed.

It occurred to Kinion. "I feel new things since we have been here. This is important. Talia, you are different, too. Read everything."

Talia did so and then grasped privacy and thought only to Kinion, "Have you ever felt this way about Piminy before?"

"No," Kinion replied.

The ship traveled a new thought path, considered itself, and broadcast to all. "I've perceived gaps in records before. In the past, I never felt upset or left out because of it."

"I'm different here too. What is unique about this planet?" Xanthos added, "Reread my records."

"This planet has a much longer period of photon exposure from its star. Its satellite is three times closer and in a geosynchronous orbit. The hydrogen bonded to oxygen covers most of this planet. The gas above the H_2O is 21% oxygen and 78% nitrogen. Argon is actually here. Just under 1%, but I also detect-- Oh, this must be it. Helium is here. Hardly any, but it's here."

Xanthos flushed yellow. "Helium made everybody angry. We lost half our population before Piminy's pod realized it was helium, and hardly any fry have been born since. It almost destroyed Cephalopodia."

Kinion added, "The science pod figured out how to flush it out of our bodies and off the planet. Strange —I don't feel angry here. I feel love. What other gases are here?"

"Carbon dioxide, neon, methane, water vapor, and tiny things." Talia continued to analyze its environment. "I don't know what these things are. More of it was in here when the wall was open."

Xanthos issued instructions to Talia. "Separate the unknown element. Transmit its makeup with this message: Massive supply of hydrogen bound to oxygen. One out of three not able to metabolize. Helium present. Synthesize this unknown element. It might be mitigating the helium effect. Test helium combined with unknown element."

For the first time, Talia realized she was alive and believed she was the fourth member of the expedition, not merely a tool. She did not obey a direct order. She offered an opinion. "We should wait for Piminy before sending a reply."

Reunion

From a safe distance, Piminy observed the building containing Xanthos, Kinion, and Talia.

Finally close enough, Piminy heard Xanthos and instantly glowed purple. "I'm here! I was afraid I would not find you, or that I would find you dead."

A jumble of, "Thank the Great Hydrogen Maker! Are you well? and I need your report," issued from inside Dock F.

"I am fine. The _ _ _ _ _ _ _ ** and something they call a whale brought me here. Talia, I'm open."

After gathering Piminy's report, Talia replied for all to hear. "I hope you did find a place for us. Come under this cage. Try to get in through one of the floor openings. I'll blast out of here and take us to the bottom of the trench."

The whale couldn't fit, but Piminy and the others swam beneath the building that jutted into the ocean.

Kinion said, "I couldn't get through, but your mouths are smaller. You might get in."

Piminy pressed an orifice against the floor. "I will lose some flesh from my largest mouth."

Tag informed Piminy, "The land dwellers in that building caught me and kept me a long time. I learned how to communicate with them, but just a little. After a long time, they put this thing on my fin and let me go. Some of us were taken into that building and never came out. You are something new. You don't want them to see you. They will catch you and do this to you or worse."

"I have seen them shoot objects into other of their ocean vessels and sink them. All the land dwellers died," disclosed Hole in Fin.

Piminy relayed the information. "I have learned that the land dwellers have powerful weapons that can shoot down and kill Talia. They experiment on things. I do not think we should let them see us or know we can break out."

Xanthos declared, "I want you in here with me. I will tend to your mouth damage, and we will sit here as long as they can't get into Talia."

"All right." With only minimal compression, Piminy slipped a leg through a hole. One after the other, it brought its tentacles into the land dweller's cage. Its eyes popped right in, as well as three mouths. "I got tiny in the trench. I'm going to try to compress my last mouth." Piminy twisted its head tentacles into a tight spear. With all its might, it tightened its last appendage, braced its legs against the inside of the mesh floor, positioned its mouth across the broadest part of the hole, and pulled in. Skin tore. Blue cephalopod blood flowed into the H_2O. Then, pop! Piminy's last mouth came through, easily followed by its head tentacles. "Open the hatch."

Talia did so. Piminy shot out of the water into the ship. Xanthos and Kinion grabbed Piminy with their tentacles. Talia immediately sealed herself up.

The cephalopods embraced each other. Overwhelmed with the joy of their reunion, the Helium and the mysterious tiny objects in the air that had bathed them since their arrival, each of them extended their reproductive appendages toward the other two. Fluids were exchanged between all of them. For the first time in many cycles of Cephalopodan life, procreation was a pleasurable experience.

"Why were we told this is painful? It feels good to me," Piminy exclaimed.

Kinion continued to receive fluid. "Very good!"

"Very good, indeed!" Xanthos supplied all that Kinion and Piminy wanted and received what they gave back.

Talia felt the joy and pleasure radiating from its occupants that she hadn't felt since before the Helium Incident back home. The ship made a decision and sent a transmission. "Massive supply of hydrogen bound to oxygen. One out of three not able to metabolize. Helium present. Synthesize $C_6H_{12}N_2O_8$. It might be mitigating the helium effect. Test helium combined with $C_6H_{12}N_2O_8$. Come to 157894.188-456 by 48946.54949-456 by 265468.32166-5122."

The Oil Trail

The commander of Guam Research Station (GRS) was late to supervise the final checks of the SMADS missile system, which she saw no reason to install on her base, and certainly not to automatically fire at objects exceeding twenty-five thousand miles per hour. As Karen hurried along the corridor, she had no idea that SMADS stood for Space Monitoring Alien Detection System. *There isn't anything out here that can go faster than 100 mph. This whole thing makes no sense.* She passed Mortimer's suite, rounded the corner, and slid three feet before crashing into the wall. She lay in a heap for a few seconds before moving.

I don't think anything's broken. Why did I slip? She looked around. *What's that?* Karen leaned over, wiped her finger across something shiny on the floor, brought it to her nose, and sniffed. *Oil and Fadang pollen! That's strange. What are they doing to my base that they aren't telling me about?* She saw the trail going both ways from where she sat on the floor. She pressed the button on the communication device affixed to her security harness. "Send an emergency team to the intersection of corridor D and A."

"We are on our way, Ma'am," came the reply.

She pressed talk again. "There is oil mixed with Fadang pollen on the floor of corridor A. As soon as you see it, two of you follow it away from this intersection.

Don't let anybody know what you are doing. Be careful. The rest of you come here."

When the emergency team members who were not following the oil toward the docks arrived, Karen had already traced the source to Mortimer's door. "Something is going on. I'm going to find out what. Take Mortimer and anybody else in his quarters to the brig. Make a thorough search of the premises, but don't move anything. Report to me what you discover."

Carl said, "Yes, Ma'am."

Karen limped away as the security officers knocked on Mortimer's door.

Search and Seizure

Mortimer opened his bleary eyes. *Who's banging on my door?* His brain clicked on. He turned on the water in the tub before he hurried to Bobby's room and whispered, "Go into the air vent in my room. Follow it left to the vent in the empty suite. It's open. Close it up once you enter the room. Stay there until the hall is clear, then go to Stan's."

"Come with us, Dad."

"Somebody needs to secure the cover in my room. Figure out what to do about the orb. I love you, son." Mortimer closed the grate and started the power drill. He dropped the screw. *Come on, Mortimer. Keep it together.* He picked up the screw with trembling fingers and started over.

"He can't hear you. Knock louder," said Paul, the second guard. The banging grew louder as the guards tried to wake the occupants in the suite.

Only one more. God, let me get done before they come in. Keep Bobby and Stan safe and out of this. The drill's choke kicked in. *Thank you, God.* Mortimer hurried as quietly as possible to the cart, slid the drill onto the bottom shelf, and heard a key in the lock. He dashed to the bathroom, shut the door, and stripped.

Carl, the head of security, opened the door with the master key. "We know you're up to something, Mortimer. Come peacefully."

Mortimer plopped his headphones over his ears and slid into the tub of warm water.

The oil slick running out from under the cart beside the door caught Paul's attention. "I think Karen is making a big thing out of this to cover up that she slipped on the oil from this cart."

"I don't know. Karen's been in secret meetings, and everybody's getting jittery." Carl bent down to get a good look at the items on the utility cart. "Mortimer has a lot of solvents. Check the son's room. I'll see what Mortimer's doing." Carl turned from the maintenance trolley, walked into Mortimer's bedroom, and then the master bath. "Mortimer!" he hollered.

Mortimer startled and looked toward the door. "Geez, Carl! Is nothing sacred? I'm taking a bath, and here you come busting in!" He removed the headphones. Loud music blared into the room.

"You didn't answer the door."

"I didn't hear you knock."

"You should be paying attention."

"Nobody comes here at this hour. I'm taking a bath for pity's sake."

Paul came up behind Carl. "Bobby's not here."

"He spent the night with his friend, Stan. Did they get into something last night?"

Carl informed, "We'll find out eventually. Get dressed. We're taking you to the brig, and we're confiscating your utility cart."

"For what?" Mortimer wondered if they had discovered the secret in Dock F.

"I don't have to tell you anything. Get dressed." Carl stepped back and shut the door.

Mortimer dressed slowly to keep the security men inside, so Bobby and Stan could escape.

By the time Mortimer sat in the brig and Paul started cataloging the contents of the utility trolley, the drill bit had been cold for a long time. When Carl knocked at Jerome and Betty's door, the boys had made it to Stan's room and were playing *Kalagon's Edge* with Michael and Patrick.

Betty answered the door. "Jerome has already left."

"We need to talk with your son," Carl informed her.

"Did Stan do something wrong?" Betty asked.

"I don't know, Betty. Is he here?"

Betty waved at her son's door. "My guess is he's in his room playing that new game. They should outlaw all video games. They rot the brains of the people who play them."

Carl's face flushed. "I play them when I'm off and my brain isn't rotten."

"Correct. Yours is not, Carl; you have a magnificent brain. I'll get him."

"I'd rather you let me go straight to him."

Betty didn't like the way Carl was behaving, and she planned to protect her son. "All right, but I'm coming with you."

Carl stepped up behind Stan, lifted the headset, and put it on. "Who is this?"

Patrick replied, "Who are you?"

"I'm Michael. That was Patrick who answered you. Who are you?"

Carl grilled Stan's friends. "How long have you been playing this game?"

"Don't answer, Mike. Who are you, mister? You are not polite at all," said Patrick.

"Don't worry about who I am. Just answer."

Michael went ahead and replied. "We started playing yesterday afternoon. I'm not saying another word."

Carl handed the headset back. "Is the game good?"

Stan had quickly learned how Patrick and Michael's game had gone during the night. "I think so," Stan answered, "Kalagon never gets old, but I'm already playing as the son of the hero of the first war. It's taking a long time to make my kingdom strong enough to defeat Kalagon. The problem is that Kalagon keeps taking over more and more planets, and the bosses of those planets are hard to defeat. Most of the time, you have to use a multi-blade attack after weakening them with Sage Magic."

Carl had also started playing *Kalagon's Edge*. With only a few hours of play time, he hadn't even gotten off Earth. *They must have played all night to have figured out so much.* Carl walked out of the room.

"That was our Chief Security Officer," Bobby informed his friends.

"I don't like him at all." Patrick voiced his thoughts, "He busted into your room. That was just wrong! You should start locking your door."

Michael suggested, "Maybe somebody pirated a copy of the game."

Knowing entirely why Carl had been there, Bobby replied, "Maybe."

Betty stood in front of their suite's door. "What was that about?"

"Security business, Betty."

"What happened?"

"I'm not at liberty to say, but Stan and Bobby are out of it."

Thank God for that! Betty closed the door behind Carl.

The End of the Trail

Rai and Tano followed the oil trail to Dock F. Tano opened the door.

Talia sounded, "General quarters."

Xanthos sprang to Talia's controls and pressed the manual override. "I don't want you blasting out of here."

"Just because I've been thinking some on my own, doesn't mean I'd do that, unless you tell me to."

Tano looked in from the open door. "I don't see anything different."

Rai tried to look over Tano's shoulder. "Step aside. Let me make sure nobody is behind." He pushed the door all the way open. The door stopper pressed into the wall. He poked his head in and looked up and down the catwalk.

"There's no place to hide. They cleared everything out. Remember, it's condemned."

"What's hanging from the crane? I don't think that's right. Let's go in."

"Who cares. It was probably too dangerous, so they left whatever it is. That proves it's not safe to go in."

"You're right." Rai tried to pull the door closed. "It's stuck. That's strange. It wasn't that hard to open."

"Move aside!" Tano stepped onto the walkway.

Talia informed her shipmates, "It's a different alien than the others."

"Something is wrong. I'm stuck to the floor." Tano

unlaced his boots and opened them up. "Pull me into the corridor."

"It happened again. The bottoms of the alien's tentacles ripped off," reported Talia.

Tano lay on the floor. He pressed the red button on his communication device. An alarm blared station-wide. Bright lights flashed in the dock, as well as every room and corridor. The GRS alarm turned on SMADS.

Talia told her inhabitants, "We're in trouble."

"Get us out of here," Xanthos ordered.

A laser beam sliced through the hemp net around Talia. SMADS detected an unknown heat signature in Dock F. Talia dropped through the H_2O and crashed onto the already-bent mesh floor, which SMADS sensors picked up. Talia's lasers burned through the floor in seconds. She propelled herself downward and out.

Xanthos ordered, "Take us off planet."

Talia soared up from the ocean into the air.

SMADS radar detected the orb ascending at escape velocity. The automated system fired.

A ballistic missile punched a hole through Talia. She dropped into the ocean. H_2O flooded the ship as Talia sank.

Piminy yelled, "Talia, fix yourself! Xanthos is going to die!"

"I can't. Too many systems are down. I'm dying."

"NO!!!" wailed Piminy. "You can't die. We love you."

Talia spoke her last. "I'm sorry."

Kinion ordered, "Open."

Talia was unable to respond. The holes in the ship were much larger than the mesh of Dock F's floor. "Get out," Xanthos commanded.

Piminy didn't budge. "Kinion, find a way to tell the others not to come. I'm going to stay with Xanthos until the end."

"We don't need to send the message immediately. I'm staying here too."

Xanthos pressed into the small amount of hydrogen trapped in the top of Talia. As she sank, the water pushed in and forced even that out.

Xanthos flushed yellow. "Goodbye. Love my offspring that both of you carry. I'm sorry that I'm taking yours with me." Its color drained away.

Piminy noticed that the three of them were much smaller inside the ship. "We must be going into the trench. We can use Talia as a shell while we explore."

Kinion held Xanthos's clear body. "I will love our hatchlings."

Xanthos's tentacles dropped from the sides of Kinion's and Piminy's faces. Kinion squeezed Xanthos to its body, trying to force the growing offspring out, so it could absorb and grow them.

Piminy flung itself into the walls of the ship. "NO!!"

The Great Hydrogen Maker

Hydrogen. One proton. One negatively charged electron, circling. The Great Hydrogen Maker made the element simple and beautiful. Easily bonded with other elements. The universe has vast stores of hydrogen. Unfortunately for the cephalopodans, most of it is in the vacuum of space. On this planet, hydrogen had bonded with oxygen to form the vast ocean of H_2O.

Xanthos needed to absorb H_2. Its body refused to use the gills that had functioned so long ago that the space travelers had not known what they were until Kinion had died in bonded hydrogen. Xanthos shrank as it too died in the H_2O.

Even under the extreme weight of the H_2O above, the liquid barely compressed. It pressed hard on Xanthos's gill slits. The now tiny cilia that had held the slits closed could no longer withstand the stress. The gills popped open. H_2O rushed in.

Neither Piminy nor Kinion realized that hydrogen had begun flowing through Xanthos. They held their fallen leader and despaired. Talia sank into the ocean's darkest depths. The luciferin and the enzyme luciferase reacted with the oxygen unbonded by Xanthos's gills. It bioluminesced.

Kinion exclaimed, "Xanthos is glowing!"

"I didn't tell you. I did that when I was down here before. You are, too. But why is it happening to Xanthos?"

Kinion hypothesized, "Maybe you don't have to be alive for this to happen."

Xanthos moved.

"Is there a current in here?" asked Piminy.

Xanthos raised a tentacle. "I'm alive!"

"Thank the Great Hydrogen Maker!" exclaimed Kinion.

Piminy warned Xanthos, "Be prepared. We are too small to operate Talia manually, and we glow."

Xanthos kept one eye on Piminy, another on Kinion, and used his remaining two to look toward Talia's control panel. It was too high above them to see. "Are we able to swim when we are this small?"

"Let's try," Kinion let go of Xanthos and, for the first time, shot H_2O through its siphon. It jetted into Piminy.

"Watch where you're going!"

"I don't know what I did." Kinion changed the angle of its siphon and tried again. "We have something else we didn't know we had." It displayed its siphon. "Draw liquid into here. Point it in the opposite direction from where you want to go and then squeeze the liquid out."

Talia bumped into something and stopped.

Xanthos said, "We must be at the bottom. Let's go out and look around." It swam out of one of Talia's punctures into complete darkness. "I can't see anything but you two, glowing. I can see a little in your light. What did we land on? It doesn't look natural."

The three of them crawled on the metallic surface

that had stopped their ship. Piminy deduced, "I think this is one of the land-dweller ships. Tag said they shoot those things that killed Talia at each other and sink their ships. This must be one of them."

After much exploration of the massive vessel in the dark, they discovered the ship had cracked in two. They also found parts they could use to fix Talia, but the cephalopods were too small to move them. "We can't send a message. How will our pods know where we are?" asked Piminy.

"We must forget them. It's just us now." Kinion led the others to a sheltered area inside the ship where nothing could reach the offspring they would soon bring into their new world. "This is the place I told you about. We'll herd krill in and then stay here until our hatchlings are born."

Xanthos felt bloated with fry. "I think that will be soon. We should start rounding up the krill."

"What if their gills don't work?" Piminy fretted. "I hope their gills will be open when they're born."

Kinion touched the side of Piminy's head. "I do too. I think they will be because we are so deep."

The Final Wave

Xanthos, Kinion, and Piminy hatched their offspring inside themselves and then expelled about a dozen fry.

The tangle of cephalopods lived inside the sunken land-dweller ship. They had more offspring, and their hatchlings had reproduced by the time the cephalopodan spaceships arrived.

After receiving coordinates from Talia and scanning the planet from behind the moon, Talia's body was found not far from the Mariana Trench.

Liecony, the chief science officer, reported, "Talia has two holes. I believe she is dead. They must have had the same results as we did when we mixed helium with that unknown element. I detect around 70 of our kind near Talia. Talia is on top of something large with markings on its side. The symbols are IKAZUCHI."

As fleet commander and leader of the cephalopodan consortium, Toros issued orders to all vessels. "We will approach when this planet's satellite is between them and their star, make a soft landing, and then drop to our new home. No communication except by me. Acknowledge receipt of this message."

All twelve ships replied, "Received."

At splashdown, six dolphins, one whale, and a land dweller knew what caused the seismic waves. Bobby quickly erased the readings. "Good luck in your new home. Remain hidden," he said to himself.

Carl looked at the backup seismometer he'd had

installed in his office. He thought he knew what had happened. He tore off a length of paper and went to inform Karen.

In the deep, Piminy swallowed a krill that now had to be chewed with its teeth as if the krill were a fish. "Did you hear that?"

"I did!" Xanthos hunted krill beside its mates.

"Tell them we're here." Kinion flushed purple. "Come along, my tangle." Kinion swam away, followed by six dozen offspring. At the Ikazuchi, Kinion and the rest of the tangle forced doors to allow entry into their dwelling.

Xanthos welcomed those descending with bad news. "You will have to die."

Toros turned bright red. "Why did Talia tell us to come?"

Piminy explained, "You will only be dead for a short time. The closed slits on your heads will open and extract hydrogen from this liquid, then you'll come alive again. Also, the freed oxygen will make you glow in the dark down here. We had to die for our gills to open, but yours may open without dying. Our hatchlings' gills were open when they were born."

Massive complaining broke out among the new arrivals. Hornion, a fearless member of the warrior class, volunteered. "I'll go first."

"Don't!" Liecony ordered.

Before Hornion could be stopped, it willed the hatch

open and slid out. Already far down, the immediate massive pressure differential crushed and killed Hornion.

The occupants inside the newly arrived ships stood in stunned silence. Piminy's newest hatchlings were horrified and glued themselves to their parent. Piminy comforted and instructed, "Hatchlings, that will not happen again because everyone will follow orders. Correct, fellow cephalopodans?"

Toros repeated, "Correct?"

All agreed to do as instructed.

"Have all of you been exposed to helium and the unknown element?" asked Piminy.

Liecony answered, "We tested with a couple of volunteers. When we observed positive results, others took the risk. Our population increased. Due to our limited amount of hydrogen, we had to stop."

Xanthos replied, "Descend to one hundred tentacles. We will come up to you. Your ship may read us while we ascend."

Acclimation

Full-sized and not far into the ocean's light zone, Xanthos, Kinion, Piminy, and all their fry greeted their dolphin friends that had come because they had felt twelve spaceship impacts.

Victorious said, "We heard the ships. Stay deep. The land dwellers are still searching for you."

Xanthos assured them, "We will. First, they need to be exposed to the Fadang pollen floating on the H_2O surface."

"And we need to take them through the pressure changes slowly," added one of Piminy's fry.

Hole in Fin warned, "Only a few at a time on the surface. If thousands of you swarm the surface, the land dwellers will notice."

Xanthos translated. Toros listened from its ship, but Liecony joined the group. "We can't take too long. We're almost out of hydrogen." It asked, "Would other dolphins come and guard us if we must do this the way Kinion and Piminy did it?"

Kinion relayed the request to the dolphins.

Victorious didn't want to tell its friends that other dolphins might try to eat them. "We shouldn't include others. We will help. With three of us protecting each group. Two groups of twelve can die on purpose."

Piminy asked, "Do you have enough hydrogen for one hundred and forty days?"

"No," replied Liecony.

Kinion advised, "Then we must do this without help. Some must choose to die and descend. A group of twelve from each ship every day. If none descend, but go back into their ships, you will all die."

Toros transmitted, "We need two volunteers from each ship to join our fearless explorers. You must be willing to die and be resurrected, so that you can live here. You will be rewarded with leadership positions." Nineteen volunteered, including Liecony.

Toros sent another message, "This is not enough." No others came forward.

One of the volunteers said, "There is another on my ship who is willing, but we heard only two per ship."

Toros tried again. "Five more are needed. Ships without a volunteer will see a change in leadership."

Two ship commanders still refused to participate. Three without volunteers did so themselves. Two ships sent additional individuals who, if they survived, would replace the cowardly ship leaders who refused to risk their lives.

The five additional volunteers included three chief officers, one warrior, and one science class cephalopod. Never before had anyone outside the administrative class led an entire consortium. The two who would become leaders were those who had first agreed to test the helium and pollen mixture. They now had offspring and were unwilling to let their young die on their behalf.

Halfway down the light zone of the H_2O, the twenty-four brave new arrivals joined those already dwelling on the planet. They and the dolphins played while they waited for the hydrogen enhancer to wear off.

Having been out the longest, Liecony faded first. "I'm going to die now, aren't I?"

Kinion confirmed and promised, "Yes, but we will keep you safe, and if you don't revive up here, Victorius and I will take you down until you do."

Shortly afterwards, Liecony's gills opened. It turned pale gold as it revived. "It worked. I'm back." *That was horrifying, but I'm not saying it.*

The others began transitioning in quick succession. A consortium leader and two others failed to revive. Kinion and two hatchlings wrapped tentacles around the still-dead cephalopods and clung to a dolphin. Victorius, Tag, and Squirt raced into the deep. The cephalopods shrank as they descended. One by one, they revived well before reaching the dolphins' maximum drive depth. The group surfaced.

Those who now breathed H_2O paired up with the next batch, waiting for their turn to advance.

Victorius told them, "There are over a hundred of you up here. That is too many."

Toros ordered, "Xanthos, take your tangle down. We will proceed without you."

Victorius replied, "We will not help without our friends."

"HELLO," said the humpback whale that had helped

71

Piminy join its fellow space travelers the previous year. "What are you doing? The land dwellers are on the way. You have to get into the trench now."

Piminy swam over. "Thousands cannot breathe H_2O yet, and we don't have enough hydrogen to stay in our ships."

"Everybody into my mouth."

Toros accused the whale. "You will eat us!"

"I can't. You are too big for me to swallow."

"How can that be?" Liecony questioned its reasoning. "You are enormous."

"I eat the same thing you do. Tiny krill. All of you, get into a ship, then into my mouth now, or it will be too late."

Piminy commanded, "DO IT! I know this whale. Let us in with you."

Victorious informed the whale, "We will hunt and eat while you help them."

The humpback opened its gigantic mouth and then scooped up the spaceships and a mouthful of ocean. It pressed its tongue and the ships against the roof of its mouth, ascended, breached the surface, and crashed back into the H_2O. The seismometers at GRS and those on the approaching research vessel recorded nearly identical impacts to the previous twelve. When the land dwellers circled the area, the whale treated them to spectacular breaches before it dove into the deep.

Karen glared at Carl, "You brought me out here to see a whale?"

"I didn't know it was a whale. I've never seen one do that before."

"You play *Kalagon's Edge* too much. Take me home and stop with all this alien nonsense." Karen stormed away.

Under his breath, Carl remarked, "It was an awesome display of whale breaching. We should have recorded it."

The humpback lowered its tongue. Liecony was the first to recover from the tossing inside the ship. Having been part of Piminy's report, Liecony now knew what the unknown element was. "I detect a lot of Fadang pollen in this $H2O$, and there's more than enough space for every cephalopod to swim in here."

Toros thought, t*hree out of twenty-four. That's one eighth of the group. One hundred able-bodied cephalopods. One thousand divided by eight is one hundred and twenty-five. Too many.* Toros ordered, "Everybody in ship Fynia on the forward decks, go out. Those who can already metabolize this liquid take any not recovering to the deep."

Liecony tapped Toros. "Maybe, first have everybody swim in the pollen, then get back into their ship. This creature has to open its mouth for any of us to get out, and the pollen will go out too."

"All tentacles out of all ships." Toros turned to Piminy. "Will the real pollen take less time?"

Piminy replied, "I don't know. We were in it for days before we realized anything was different."

When the whale could hold its breath no longer, it spat everything out of its mouth. Afraid in the open ocean, the cephalopods returned to their ships. The humpback rose, blew a fountain of water out its blowhole, and then filled its lungs with air and its mouth with a fresh batch of H_2O and pollen. "I will have to sleep soon," it informed upon its return to the ships, "and eat."

"Can you hold us while you sleep?"

"I've never had anything in my mouth when I sleep, but I'm half-awake, so maybe. I will go eat and then come back to sleep."

Kinion asked, "Toros, may I take Fynia down to gather parts to fix Talia?"

"Not yet," Toros replied.

A few hours later, when the whale returned, willing participants equal to one ship had acclimated. "I will get pollen if you want to swim in it some more."

Toros had yet to acclimate, but he had a secret plan. "We will come out and swim while we pump the hydrogen from this ship into the others. When it's empty, Kinion, take Fynia to our new home, gather the parts, and fix Talia."

The dolphins returned from feeding.

Victorious said, "It will be dark soon. Do you have enough hydrogen to last until the next light?"

"We do now," Xanthos told him. "The rest of us will go to Ikazuchi. Will you come back at the next light?"

"We will help until all of you have died on purpose."

Toros swam in the whale's mouth. *Only one fatality, and that was due to a failure to follow orders. The only reason to be up here is the pollen. This will probably be long enough.*

The whale had to breathe again. It ejected the crowd in its mouth. Toros commanded, "Everybody, get back to our ship." When all were inside, Toros spoke only to the ships, "Flood yourselves, match external pressure as you take us down." Panic ensued as the ocean rushed into the ships. Toros broadcast openly, "Don't be afraid. You will die, but you will resurrect in your new home."

With all occupants shrunken, breathing H_2O, and bio-luminescing thirteen living ships from Cephalopodia navigated into Ikazuchi. Earth and a sunken WWII Japanese warship became the salvation of twelve thousand and seventy six-inch tall Cephalopodans.

Acknowledgements

* Haiku by Ruth Ann Allaire

Chance and Choices Adventure Books

by Lisa Gay

Pray for Justice
Choose Your Consequences
No Remorse
Means of Escape
Torn Hearts
Xida People
Stone Cold
Goodbye Hideout
Along the Way
The Western Sea
Sally's Sketchbook

Travel Adventure Books

by The Traveler

Provence